Shh!
Can you
keep a secret?

You're about to meet the
Ballet Bunnies, who live hidden at
Millie's ballet school.

Are you ready?

Tiptoe this
way. . . .

Meet the Ballet Bunnies

Dolly

You'll never meet a bunny who loves to dance as much as Dolly.

Fifi

If you're in trouble, Fifi is always ready to lend a helping paw!

Pod

Pod loves to build
things out of the bits
and pieces he finds. He
also loves his tutu!

Trixie

Yawn! When she's
not dancing, Trixie
likes curling up and
having a nice snooze.

For Rodney and Beauty

Text copyright © 2021 by Swapna Reddy
Cover art and interior illustrations copyright © 2021 by Binny Talib

All rights reserved. Published in the United States by Random House Children's Books, a division of Penguin Random House LLC, New York. Originally published in paperback by Oxford University Press, Oxford, in 2021.

Random House and the colophon are registered trademarks and A Stepping Stone Book and the colophon are trademarks of Penguin Random House LLC.

Visit us on the Web!
rhcbooks.com

Educators and librarians, for a variety of teaching tools, visit us at
RHTeachersLibrarians.com

Library of Congress Cataloging-in-Publication Data is available upon request.
ISBN 978-0-593-30572-0 (pbk.) — ISBN 978-0-593-30573-7 (lib. bdg.) —
ISBN 978-0-593-30574-4 (ebook)

MANUFACTURED IN CHINA
10 9 8 7 6 5 4 3 2 1
First American Edition 2021

This book has been officially leveled by using the
F&P Text Level Gradient™ Leveling System.

Random House Children's Books supports the First Amendment
and celebrates the right to read.

Ballet  Bunnies

The Lost Slipper

By Swapna Reddy

Illustrated by Binny Talib

A STEPPING STONE BOOK™
Random House ⌂ New York

Chapter 1

"I can't believe we're here!" Millie giggled with glee. Her ballet class from Miss Luisa's School of Dance was on a trip to the theater to see a ballet production of *Cinderella*.

"It's exciting, isn't it?" Auntie Karen said, grinning at everyone. Millie's favorite

aunt was one of the grown-up helpers on
the trip.

Millie looked up at Auntie Karen, whose
long hair was pulled back to reveal sparkly

diamond earrings. As the earrings twinkled, Millie couldn't help but be reminded of Cinderella all dressed up for the ball.

The entrance to the theater filled with noise as more people gathered, ready for the show to start. Auntie Karen stepped back. Millie followed and carefully picked up her feet so that her new shoes wouldn't get scuffed and trampled by the crowd.

Millie giggled again as the light streaming in through the open doors caught on her shoes. Auntie Karen had given her a beautiful pair of sparkly shoes that looked exactly like Cinderella's glass slippers. Millie tippy-tapped her feet on the theater

floor, and the shoes glittered on the deep red carpet.

"They are just like the real glass slippers," Auntie Karen said, smiling down at Millie.

Millie hugged her aunt tight. *Cinderella* was one of her favorite stories. It was the

first book Auntie Karen had ever read to her. They read it almost every night when Auntie Karen stayed over.

Millie knew the story by heart. She could shut her eyes and imagine dancing her way across the words. She could see Cinderella leaving her awful life with her stepfamily as she's transformed into a beautiful princess by her fairy godmother. She could see Cinderella and the Prince waltzing across the palace floor. And she could see poor Cinderella accidentally leaving one of her glass slippers behind as she rushed home.

The whole story felt so magical to Millie.

She wished that one day her dream of dancing the part of Cinderella onstage would come true.

Millie squeezed Auntie Karen's hand tight and saw her special shoes catch the light again, but this time she was sure she saw the sparkles flutter and dance.

Everything had a way of being magical when Auntie Karen was around.

Chapter 2

"Oh, bunny fluff! Is it almost time to take our seats?"

The tiny head and long ears of a golden-haired bunny popped out from the inside pocket of Millie's coat.

"What was that?" Auntie Karen said, turning to look at Millie.

"Oh, nothing, Auntie Karen," Millie
said, pulling her coat tightly around her and
shielding the little bunny from sight.

"That's an awfully big coat, Millie," Auntie Karen said. "You look more ready for a polar expedition than an afternoon at the theater." She reached out to Millie. "Can I take it for you?"

"No!" Millie said, holding on tight to her coat. Seeing Auntie Karen's startled face, Millie quickly added, "I'm actually really cold."

The truth was she was really too hot. She couldn't wait to take off her coat and tuck it under her seat. But she had to hold on to it for now because of the four little bunnies who were hiding in her pockets.

Four little Ballet Bunnies.

Dolly, Fifi, Trixie, and Pod, the resident Ballet Bunnies at Miss Luisa's School of Dance, had snuck into Millie's large coat before she climbed on board the bus. There was no way they were going to miss the chance to see *Cinderella*!

As the bunnies squirmed, Millie wiggled around under the weight of the coat, hoping to hide her furry friends from Auntie Karen. Millie had forgotten the hole in her left pocket that the bunnies were now using as a warren to travel to each other. Every now and then the coat would sag to one side as all four bunnies snuck into the same pocket!

"Oh, I hope we get good seats," Millie
heard Fifi exclaim to the other bunnies.

"Hold on!" Pod said. "Are you in the same pocket as me, Fifi? It's hard to tell in the dark."

"Yes, I am!" Fifi said. "I was getting a little bored in mine all on my own."

"I'm in here too now," Dolly said. "I've got nothing but a seashell in my pocket, and I thought I could smell a couple of mints that Millie had snuck away in this pocket."

"Where's Trixie?" Pod asked.

The bunnies fell silent so the faint snores of Trixie in Millie's top pocket could be heard.

"That means we are all on the same

side of Millie's coat!" Pod said. "We have to get back to our own pockets. Otherwise,

someone might wonder why Millie's coat looks lopsided."

As the bunnies scampered back across their padded warren, Millie straightened up, relieved that Auntie Karen hadn't noticed her wriggling coat.

Chapter 3

People started to swarm the open doors and walk into the auditorium, searching for their seats. Millie could feel herself being pushed this way and that. To protect the bunnies, she stepped away from the crowd and watched as her ballet class

and Auntie Karen moved ahead of her.

She reached out for her aunt's hand but was tipped over by the weight of her coat.

"My shoe!" Millie gasped.

She looked down at her feet, where only one shoe twinkled. Panic grew in her chest.

"Don't worry, Millie," Dolly cried.

"We'll help you find it."

The four bunnies hopped out of their pockets and scrambled to the ground, careful not to be seen.

Millie dropped to the carpet on all fours, searching between ankles in the darkness. Her chest felt tight at the thought of having to tell Auntie Karen that she had lost one of her shoes.

She watched Pod as he darted across the carpet ahead of her, his long ears tall and straight as he searched for the slipper. He

dodged between people's feet, careful not to be stepped on as the throng of theater-goers made their way inside.

Millie's eyes filled with tears. What would she tell Auntie Karen? She hated the idea of disappointing her favorite aunt.

"Millie! Over here!" Fifi said.

Millie's heart leapt with hope as she dashed over to where the bunnies had gathered.

"Here," Fifi said, frantically waving her paw. She pointed at a gap under a closed door. "I have a feeling that your slipper might be through here."

Chapter 4

"Wait!" Millie cried when the bunnies leaned against the door, ready to push it open.

Millie bit her lip and peered around.

"I don't think we should go in there," she said.

"But we need to get your shoe!" Dolly
exclaimed.

"I'm still not sure we should go in there," Millie replied.

Dolly tugged on Millie's coat. "We'll just open the door and grab your shoe," she said eagerly. "We'll be sitting down ready for the performance before you know it."

Millie wrung her hands. She had to admit Dolly did make a good point.

"I could try to squeeze under the door," Pod suggested.

Millie knelt and peered beneath the door. She could see something glinting. Could it be her shoe? She reached her hand through the gap, her arm scraping the bottom of the door. The shoe was just out of reach.

She nodded at Pod as she pulled away from the door. "Please try, but be careful."

The little bunny smoothed back the tuft of dark fur over his eye and flicked back his ears. He burrowed his way under the door, wriggling his bottom and flattening himself against the floor.

"Give me a push," he called back to the bunnies.

"Be careful, Pod," Millie cried.

Fifi, Dolly, and Trixie pushed Pod farther under the door, but it was no good. They writhed and squirmed and shoved and heaved. Pod was trapped!

"I'm stuck!" Pod yelped.

"We know!" the bunnies chimed back as they stopped pushing to catch their breath.

Millie rushed forward and nestled in close to Pod. She stroked his soft fur over his hind legs. "Are you okay, Pod?"

"Yes," Pod replied, "but I would rather not be stuck under this door. My nose is itchy, and I can't reach to scratch it."

"I could try to go under and push Pod

out the other way," Trixie suggested. "I am the smallest of us."

"No!" Millie said. "I will not lose another bunny under this door."

She got to her feet and dusted off her coat.

"We'll have to open the door," Dolly said. "It's the only way to get Pod out."

Millie twisted the handle gently. The door opened with a click.

"Well?" Dolly said, her eyes sparkling with excitement. "Are we going to see what's on the other side?"

Millie glanced back at the theater entrance. The crowd was still moving

toward the auditorium. She spotted the
rest of her ballet class, chatting excitedly
and completely unaware that Millie wasn't
with them.

She caught Auntie Karen's eye. She
opened her mouth to call out to her, when
Auntie Karen turned away. But not before

giving Millie a smile and a wink as though she were giving Millie her blessing.

Millie shut her mouth and looked down at the bunnies.

"I guess we're going through the door, then," she said.

Chapter 5

The door swung open, and Millie scooped up Pod as he shimmied free.

She and the bunnies found themselves in a backstage corridor.

"It's magical," Dolly gasped.

The walls sparkled and the floor

glittered. Millie felt sure she was in a place full of enchantment and dreams.

The hallway was flanked by footmen dressed in red velvet jackets lined with gold braid. Their big shiny buttons caught the light and reflected a glittery pattern on the walls.

Dancers darted from room to room, gathering their

costumes and stretching before the show.

"Welcome," said one of the footmen, bowing to Millie as though he had been expecting her.

Millie tucked Pod in close to her, and Fifi, Dolly, and Trixie darted behind her legs.

"And hello to you too, bunnies," the footman said, kneeling down to tickle the hiding bunnies under their chins.

Millie stared in awe as, one by one, dancers rushing by stopped to greet her and the bunnies. It was as though she had opened the door into a magical bubble where it was completely normal for four bunnies to be hopping around backstage as ballet dancers got ready.

Millie watched as the dancers warmed up, and she listened as the orchestra beneath the stage tuned their instruments. Millie's heart felt full at the idea that perhaps one day *she* would be stretching and tying on her ballet shoes, ready to dance in *Cinderella*.

"Look at me! I'm Cinderella," Dolly sang as she danced down the corridor, skipping between the props waiting to be placed on the stage.

The little bunny had grabbed a piece of loose fabric and pirouetted with it in front of the painted backdrop for the palace ball. The taffeta wrapped around Dolly like a huge ball gown. Fifi leapt high and landed a grand jeté, before bowing like a prince.

Millie laughed along with the bunnies and ran her fingers gently over the crushed velvet and crystals on the palace thrones.

She wished she could dance and jeté on the dreamy stage just once, but her wishful thinking was interrupted.

A dancer rushed over to Millie. "We have something for you," she said.

As the performers gathered around

Millie and the bunnies, the footman reappeared alongside the dancer.

He bent down and held out four tiny footmen costumes, complete with gold braiding and miniature gold buttons.

"These are for you," he said to the bunnies.

"Oh, bunny fluff," Dolly gasped. "They are beautiful!"

The bunnies took their costumes and thanked the footman, rushing off to try them on.

The footman straightened up and looked at Millie. "I see you are all ready for the show."

Millie peered down and saw that her clothes had magically transformed into a white sparkly tutu made of the softest tulle and delicate crystals. On her feet were pink ballet slippers.

"It's beautiful," Millie gasped. "How—"

Before anyone could answer, the dancers bustled around Millie.

"Hurry," a dancer said. "We need you all in your costumes onstage."

Chapter 6

Millie quickly swept up her hair and rushed to the stage.

The curtains were down, and Millie could hear the excitement of the crowd on the other side as they took their seats, rustling their programs.

"Can you believe we are on the set of *Cinderella*?" Dolly squealed.

The bunnies looked adorable in their outfits, and Millie felt like Cinderella at the ball in her beautiful, perfectly fitted tutu.

"I can't go onstage," Millie cried.

"Oh, bunny fluff," Fifi replied. "Of course you can."

"I can't," Millie said, cowering and edging backward. "I'm not good enough to be on the set of *Cinderella*."

The bunnies looked at each other and then smiled up at Millie. "We can't think of anyone better to play Cinderella," Pod said. "It's your dream, remember?"

Millie *did* remember but still thought she wasn't good enough to be there.

"Shall we dance?" came a voice from behind them.

A ballerina dressed in the exact same tutu as Millie pirouetted onto the stage. She was the most beautiful dancer Millie had ever seen. Her long hair was tied up high on her head in a bun, and she wore sparkly diamond earrings that looked very familiar.

With the curtains down, she leapt high, then spun across the stage, keeping perfect time. Millie couldn't take her eyes off the beautiful dancer.

"Let's dance!" Dolly cried, taking Trixie's paw and spinning her.

The bunnies pirouetted in unison across the stage, just like the ballerina.

"And how about you, Millie?" asked the dancer, holding out a hand.

"I'm not as good as you are," Millie said, unsure.

"Believe in yourself," the ballerina whispered gently. "This is your time to shine."

Millie took the ballerina's hand and followed her lead. When she felt a tug at her hand, she leapt up high, and when she felt a squeeze, she pirouetted in time with the others as though she had been doing this for years and years. She even managed to dance en pointe—on the tips of her toes—twirling like the tiny doll in her music box. She felt like she was flying in a wonderful dream.

The bunnies cheered and squealed with delight as Millie danced around the stage.

"Millie, you are just like Cinderella!"
Dolly cried.

"How am I able to do this?" Millie gasped. She beamed from ear to ear, unable to contain the joy that came from realizing her dreams.

The ballerina smiled at Millie and gathered the bunnies around.

"I can tell that you want to be a real ballerina one day," she said to Millie. She threw her arms open. "This could all be yours if you work hard." She winked at the bunnies. "And a little bit of magic is always handy."

"Who are you?" Millie asked.

Fifi gasped. "Oh, Millie, she's your fairy godmother!"

The dancer smiled again as the orchestra fell silent and the stage went dark.

"It's time to go, Millie," she said gently. "The show is about to start." And with that she handed Millie her missing slipper.

Chapter 7

Millie and the bunnies had completely forgotten the time and their mission to rescue Millie's shoe!

The ballerina and the footman linked arms with Millie. The bunnies scampered ahead as they all ran toward the door, rushing to get off the stage.

"Where will you go?" Millie asked
the bunnies. She was sure that by now
the entrance to the theater would be

clear of the crowd. If she and the bunnies were to go back, they would be seen. She was also sure that on the other side of the doors, four talking bunnies wouldn't be quite so safe.

"Don't worry," the footman reassured Millie. "I'll find them the best seats in the house."

"Let's get you to the auditorium, Millie," the ballerina said.

Millie quickly hugged each of the bunnies and watched as they scurried off with the footman in the opposite direction.

Then she went with the ballerina, down the corridor toward the door. She opened the door and stepped through to the familiar red-carpeted entryway. She turned to look down the corridor and take in the magic one last time.

But the corridor was empty.

Millie craned her neck, trying to spot a footman in a flash of red and gold. But no. There were no footmen to be seen. She stepped forward, hoping to see a dancer or two stretching, ready to go onstage. But no. There were no dancers anywhere.

"Where did everyone go?" Millie asked, turning back to the ballerina.

Her mouth fell open when she saw that the ballerina was no longer there. Instead, peering down at her with a mischievous

grin, was Auntie Karen, as though she had been with Millie the whole time.

"Auntie Karen!" Millie exclaimed. "Where did the ballerina go?"

"What ballerina?" Auntie Karen asked.

"The ballerina who was right here," Millie insisted.

Auntie Karen swung around to search

everywhere. She cupped a hand above her eyes, pretending to look high and low like the captain of a ship.

"It's just us, Millie," Auntie Karen said, smiling. Her hair was tucked behind her ears, where Millie noticed a very familiar pair of earrings twinkling in the light.

Chapter 8

Auntie Karen hugged Millie close as Millie's brow wrinkled in confusion.

"But, Auntie Karen, I was on the stage just now, behind the curtain," she said.

She told her auntie all about the magical corridor and the footmen with their jackets trimmed in gold braid. She told her about the ballerina and how they had danced together, flying through the air and spinning on the tips of their toes.

"Oh, Auntie Karen, it was magical," Millie said, twirling on the spot. "I even wore an extra-special tutu to match the ballerina. See?"

She stood up straight so that Auntie Karen could admire her sparkly tutu.

Auntie Karen nodded admiringly. "It's a very fine coat, Millie. Though I think a tutu is a bit of a stretch."

Millie peered down and saw that she was indeed back in her usual clothes.

"But my tutu—" Millie started, confused.

"Your tutu sounded wonderful," Auntie
Karen reassured her. "You must have had a
very special time."

"It was very special," Millie agreed with a small smile. Millie realized then that everything she'd just seen must have been fairy-tale magic, and her heart felt heavy with sadness.

She was so disappointed to see that her beautiful tutu had vanished and that she was back in her giant coat.

Tears rolled down her face.

Auntie Karen wrapped her arms around Millie and squeezed tight. She crouched down and brushed away Millie's tears.

As Millie nestled into her auntie's warm hug, she looked down and spotted her new shoes on her feet. They twinkled and sparkled, and Millie couldn't stop the smile stretching across her face. Her auntie was very special.

"You are just like a fairy godmother, Auntie Karen," Millie said.

Chapter 9

"Please take your seats. The show is about to start," came the final call.

Millie and Auntie Karen rushed to their seats, where the rest of Millie's ballet class was waiting.

Millie squeezed in next to her friend

Samira, and they giggled with excitement as the orchestra started up.

As music filled the theater and the curtains parted, Millie was swept away in the enchantment of the ballet.

When the show finished and the dancers took their final curtsies and bows, Millie jumped to her feet and applauded harder than she had ever done before. It was the most magical thing she had ever seen.

She wiggled her toes in her shoes and remembered dancing on that very stage earlier in the day. She wondered if her magical adventure had really happened.

Millie said goodbye to her ballet class as they made their way to the exit.

She and Auntie Karen waited to the very end, until the theater was completely empty, soaking up every last second of their special day together.

As Millie waited for Auntie Karen to finish in the bathroom, she called out gently to the bunnies.

"Millie!" Dolly cried, hopping over with the others. "Wasn't that the most wonderful show?"

"It really was," Millie beamed.

"We had the best seats in the house!" Fifi squealed. "We watched the whole ballet from the thrones in the palace ballroom on the stage!"

Millie's mouth fell open. She thought she'd spotted four pairs of familiar-looking bunny ears during the ballroom scene!

She was about to scoop up the bunnies and place them in her pockets, when she stopped.

The bunnies lined up in front of her were still in their red-and-gold footmen jackets!

"Your jackets!" Millie exclaimed.

"We get to keep them," Pod said, standing up tall. "Isn't that great?"

Millie's time on the stage had happened after all!

"Let's go home, Millie," Auntie Karen called.

As Millie quickly placed each of the bunnies in her pockets, she looked back at her auntie in her sparkly earrings.

The air really had been filled with fairy-godmother magic.

Basic ballet moves

First position

Second position

Third
position

Fourth
position

Fifth position

Glossary of ballet terms

Arabesque—Standing on one leg, the
dancer extends the other leg
out behind them.

Barre—A horizontal bar at waist
level on which ballet dancers rest
a hand for support during certain
exercises.

Demi-plié—A small bend of the knees, with
heels kept on the floor.

En pointe—Dancing on the very tips of the
toes.

Grand jeté—A leap in which the dancer
throws one leg forward and the other leg
backward, so that they are in a full split
in midair.

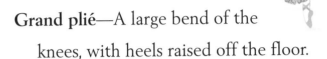

Grand plié—A large bend of the knees, with heels raised off the floor.

Jeté—A leap in which the dancer throws one leg to the front, side, or back.

Pas de deux—A dance for two people.

Pirouette—A spin made on one foot, turning all the way around.

Plié—A movement in which the dancer bends the knees and straightens them again while the feet are turned out and heels are kept on the floor.

Relevé—A movement in which the dancer rises on the tips of the toes.

Sauté—A jump off both feet, landing in the same position.

Twirl and spin with the Ballet Bunnies in another adventure!

Turn the page for a sneak peek.

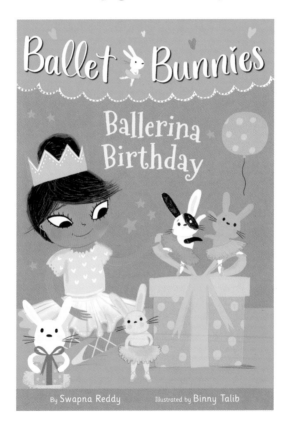

Mom stopped suddenly and spun around to look behind them. Millie turned to see that Fifi and Pod had darted behind a nearby tree trunk to stand as still as statues.

"Mom?" Millie started. She bounced nervously from foot to foot and held on to Trixie a little tighter.

Mom shook her head and turned back. "I thought someone was behind us." Mom shrugged and continued skipping beside Millie all the way to their front door.

◦ ✳ ◦

"That was close!" Dolly said. She scrambled out of Millie's bag the moment the four bunnies were safely in Millie's bedroom.

Pod picked out a leaf from his fur. "I told you we should have hidden behind that mailbox, Fifi."

"Oh, bunny fluff," Fifi said dismissively. "We're all here now, aren't we?"

Discover more magic in these page-turning adventures!

For the totally
unique ballerina!

For the
unicorn-obsessed!

For dog lovers
and budding pirates!

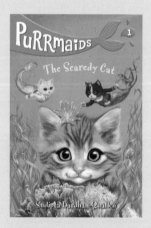

For cat lovers and
wannabe mermaids!

Find these books and more at rhcbooks.com!